I0458145

Where Trouble Roams

Janet McNulty

This is a work of fiction. Names, characters, places, and incidents within are the product of the author's imagination or are used fictitiously, and any resemblance to actual persons, living or dead, business establishments, events, or location is entirely coincidental. The publisher does not have any control over and does not assume any responsibility for author or third-party websites or their content.

Where Trouble Roams

Copyright © 2013 Janet McNulty
Cover Illustration by Robert Henry

ISBN-13: 978-0615808857
ISBN-10: 0615808859

All rights reserved.
No part of this book may be reproduced, scanned, or distributed in any printed or electronic form without permission. Please do not participate in or encourage piracy of copyrighted materials in violation of the author's rights. Purchase only authorized editions.

Printed in the United States of America

If you purchased this book without a cover, you should be aware that this book is stolen property. It was reported as "unsold and destroyed" to the publisher, and neither the author nor the publisher has received any payment for this "stripped book".

Where Trouble Roams

—For any who have ever wanted to go on a treasure hunt.

CHAPTER 1

I drummed my fingers on the steering wheel of the car as the state trooper approached. Jackie fidgeted a bit. "Will you stop?" I hissed at her.

"I can't help it. Cops make me nervous."

"You aren't nervous around Detective Shorts."

"Yeah, well he has saved our bacon a few times. Besides, it's your fault we got pulled over."

"You're the one that wanted to take my car," I said.

Last Christmas, I totaled my car while trying to escape from a murderer. As a favor, Tiny and his friends bought me a brand new car. Of course, they decided to "fix" it for me by painting it black with flames on the hood and the sides with the silhouette of a naked woman. They also added the playboy bunny on the trunk and put a small figurine on the hood of a naked woman, which would constitute as two naked women total on my car.

On the back roads of South Dakota, this car stands out. So naturally, when you are only doing five over the limit and you're the only one on the road you get pulled over.

"License and registration," said the state trooper as he reached the driver's window.

I handed him my driver's license and car registration without delay.

"Vermont, huh? What brings you out here?"

"We're on vacation," I said.

"Do you know why I pulled you over?"

Why do cops always ask that? As though it took a genius to figure it out. "Because I was speeding," I said trying to keep the sarcasm out of my voice.

The state trooper gave me a reproachful look. He handed me a ticket. "Next time, slow down."

I just took the ticket and muttered, "Yes, officer."

"They must be desperate to meet their quota," said Jackie once the cop had left.

My Aunt Ethel had sent Jackie and I brochures for the Skagway Ranch; a sort of dude ranch for city folk to experience the "Old West". Actually, it was more of a tourist trap for people who spent way too much time in the city or had nothing better to do. Right up my aunt's ally.

Since I knew there would be no turning my aunt down we accepted. Also, I was only taking one class this semester: an independent study course. My professor didn't mind me taking off as long as I emailed her updates about my project.

I turned on the lone, dirt road that my aunt's directions indicated. Almost immediately, my left, front wheel hit a pot hole. Great, there went the shock absorbers.

"How far does this go?" asked Jackie.

"No idea," I said, looking at the miles of grass in every direction, except for where the mountains loomed over us. A few, lone trees dotted the landscape as though they had just decided to plant their roots there for lack of anything else to do

Where were the people?

"I see it," exclaimed Jackie. She pointed at the sign that indicated we had entered the ranch.

I turned the car onto the second gravel road of our trip and slowly drove along. "How far are we supposed to go?"

"No idea," said Jackie as she turned the map around.

Frowning, I just continued along the lonely stretch of dirt hoping to find some sign of civilization. Eventually we saw a white building up ahead. Figuring that was where we were to go, I headed for it pulling into the gravel parking lot.

"Is this it?" asked Jackie.

"It better be," I said, turning off the car.

I watched as others pulled up emptying suitcases from the trunks of their vehicles. I pulled our bags out of the car handing Jackie hers. "Let's find Aunt Ethel."

"Mellow, darling!" A crazy old lady in a neon pink, button up shirt, jeans, and a cowboy hat slammed into me.

Ok, so Aunt Ethel found us. I hugged my aunt and smiled. She wasn't a bad person to be around, just annoying sometimes. Or, a lot of times.

"So good of you two to make it," continued my aunt, "Well, let's get you girls checked in."

We followed my aunt to the lobby where there was a front desk. "Name?" said the lady at the desk. Her name tag said, Sal.

"Mellow Summers," I said. "My aunt—"

"Here," Sal handed me a key. "Room two sixteen. Second floor."

"You two girls go up to your room. I'll meet you outside once you're settled."

Jackie and I carried our bags up the staircase to the second floor. The lodge we seemed nice. The lobby had couches and a television which was turned to some rodeo show. And there seemed to be a cafeteria of sorts. We found room two sixteen easily and used the key to get in.

This was a real key, not a card like many modern hotels use nowadays. The lock clicked and I opened the door to a spacious room with two beds and a small bathroom to the side. A dresser and two nightstands filled the crevices and a closet next to each bed. They weren't big closets but had enough space for our things.

"At least your aunt let us bunk together," said Jackie as she plopped her suitcase on one of the beds. "Oh, no. No. No. No. I'm not wearing that."

I turned to see what Jackie referred to. On her bed was the most tacky outfit: a yellow plaid shirt with cuffs on the sleeves and old lady slacks.

I checked my bed. Sure enough, something similar laid on it. I guess Aunt Ethel had done some shopping.

"You don't have to wear it," I said.

"No way am I going to. Now, let's make a pact, Mel. This time we are here to relax."

"What do you mean?" I asked.

"Well, lately, every time we go somewhere you tend to trip over a dead body."

"Jackie," I replied, "it's not as though dead bodies fall at my feet."

I opened the closet to put Aunt Ethel's suggested outfit in there. Just as I opened the door out fell a body; landing right before my feet. So much for famous last words.

"You were saying," said Jackie as she walked up to see what had caused the noise.

"Wow," said a familiar voice, "I don't think he's breathing." Rachel had materialized right beside us.

Somehow, I had the feeling that this would prove to be a more interesting vacation than I had anticipated.

CHAPTER 2

"Mellow dear, what is taking you so—Oh!" Aunt Ethel stopped the moment she noticed the dead man on the floor. "I thought we were past all this."

I rolled my eyes. Past all this? It's not like I wanted a dead man to show up in my room.

"Better call Joe." Aunt Ethel left the room.

I soon learned that Joe was the foreman of the ranch. A no-nonsense sort of man, you didn't want to fidget around him or give him anything but straight answers. He came into the room within minutes of my aunt running to get him.

"What happened?" he demanded.

"Well," said Jackie, "there appears to be a dead guy in our room."

Joe glared at her, not appreciating her sarcasm. He inspected the body. "This appears to be Michael Evans."

"Evans?" I said, my curiosity getting the better of me.

"Arrived here two days ago. Kept to himself mostly. I better call the sheriff."

Jackie pulled out her cell phone. "You can just use my phone."

"You won't get a signal out here," said Joe. "Cell phones are useless. There is a main line in the lobby and a phone in each room. Though the one in here isn't working properly. I'll have to have a talk with Sal about putting guests in a room without a workable phone."

Joe left.

"Well, girls, it looks like we got ourselves another case." Rachel threw her arms around Jackie and me.

"Mellow darling, you have got to quit finding dead bodies," chided my aunt. "It really is a bad habit."

"What? It's not like I set out to find him. Someone put him in my closet," I blurted out.

"Well, you certainly have a habit of finding such things," continued my aunt.

"You're the one who got us these rooms."

Jackie immediately shook her head trying to get me to quiet down.

"Well, Sherriff Judson will be here in a bit," said Joe as he reentered our room; his boot clomping on the wood floor. "You all are to remain in here until he arrives. He has questions for all of you."

Within thirty minutes the sheriff arrived. He inspected Michael Evans' corpse before having the body carted out. He took all of our names before beginning the questions.

"Name?" asked Sheriff Judson.

"Mellow Summers."

"Where are you from?"

"Vermont." I handed him my driver's license. He looked it over, frowned, and gave it back to me.

"What brings you to South Dakota?"

"I'm here for a fun time," I said. My sarcasm did not go unnoticed.

"I understand that you found the body."

"Yes," I replied, "I opened my closet and he fell out."

"Fell out?"

"Made a nice loud thud," said Rachel, but only I heard her.

"Yes," I said.

"Did you touch the victim at all?"

"No."

"Did you know the victim?"

"No, this was our first meeting." I kicked myself for that response. Sarcasm and police do not go together.

"Miss Summers, I would appreciate it if you took this more seriously," said Sheriff Judson.

"Look, I don't know the man. Never met him before. I came in here to unpack my suitcase, opened the closet, and out fell a body. That is all I know."

The sheriff didn't respond to my outburst. He questioned the others with the same results. No one knew the victim, other than that his name was Michael Evans. No one knew why he was at the ranch or what he did for a living. All we knew was that he was dead and in my room.

"I guess this finishes this up," said the sheriff. "We'll dust for prints, but there is no blood or anything. My guess he was killed elsewhere and put here. You girls should have your room back by this evening."

Stay in this room. Was he nuts?

"Nice hat." Rachel flipped the sheriff's hat off of his head as he walked past her. He jerked around and glared at everyone, before picking up his hat and walking out.

"I want a new room," I told Joe.

He nodded. "There is a vacant one at the end of the hall. Help yourself."

Jackie and I grabbed our suitcases and headed straight for the other room.

After we had finished unpacking, the phone in our room rang. I answered it.

"Miss Summers?" It was Detective Shorts. "A little bird informs me that you found a body."

"How'd you—"

"I have connections. You make a few when you're in law enforcement. And your recent driving record is showing a traffic violation on it."

Damn, that was quick.

"And a Sheriff Judson called back to talk to me about both you and Jackie. Imagine my surprise when I learned that it was you who discovered the body."

"Uh, in my defense," I said, "someone put that guy in my closet."

"Stay out of it."

"Pardon?"

"You heard me, Miss Summers. Stay out of it. Let the local authorities solve this one."

"I wasn't planning to—"

"Just stay out of it," ordered Detective Shorts.

"Yes, sir," I said.

"I mean it, Miss Summers."

"I'm just here for a relaxing vacation."

The silence on the other end told me he didn't believe me. Not that I blamed him. How is one supposed to relax when a dead man turns up in their closet? And the detective knew me too well.

"See that you do," said Detective Shorts.

I hung up.

"What was that all about?" asked Jackie.

"Detective Shorts got word of the dead guy."

"Oh."

"He wants us to stay out of it."

"Doesn't he know that asking you to stay out of a murder mystery is like asking an alligator not to eat the first thing that falls in its mouth?"

The door burst open as Aunt Ethel let herself in without knocking. "A mystery! How fabulous!"

Wasn't she all upset about it a minute ago? What changed?

"I don't know who's worse. You or her," Jackie whispered in my ear.

"The chase is on," continued my aunt, "Not much is known about our unfortunate victim, but we will seek justice in his name."

"Huh?" I said.

"You're going to solve this of course," said Aunt Ethel.

"I wasn't planning—"

"Oh, nonsense, dear. That sheriff doesn't know anything. Well, it's time to eat and tomorrow we learn how to ride horses."

Aunt Ethel left all excited about me solving another case.

"Is it too late to go home?" asked Jackie.

CHAPTER 3

The next morning Jackie and I showed up at the barn in jeans and t-shirts. We told my aunt that the outfits she had bought us had suffered some unfortunate accident at breakfast. You know, the kind of accident where you rip it to shreds with a pair of scissors and stuff it in the trash can.

That morning, my aunt had signed us up for a lesson on how to properly care for horses. Sounded pleasant enough and big animals didn't frighten me. We waited with some others for the teacher to show up. Turned out that the man who was to teach us about horses was the foreman himself, Joe.

"Morning everyone," said Joe as he walked up to the corral.

I looked around at the people who had shown up. One woman, who looked to be in her early twenties, stood with a bored stance checking her fingernails. I learned that her name was Liz. She was one of those aspiring actresses from Los Angeles hoping to make it big.

"I'm only here to do research for a part," she had told me when I asked her.

It looked to me that she was learning how to freeze her butt off in designer clothes.

"Snob," muttered Jackie in my ear.

"Today we will be learning the proper way to groom a horse,'" continued Joe, "Poppy, bring everyone a horse."

A tall man with a grumpy expression went into the barn and brought a horse for each of us.

"Now," said Joe, "I want you each to pick up the brush." He raised the brush in his hand so we would know what it looked like. "And then you will carefully stroke your horse like this."

"Uh," said Liz, "That will mess up my manicure."

"You're welcome to leave," answered Joe, clearly annoyed.

I shared his sentiment.

The woman next to me held her brush at arm's length while trying to stroke her animal. She had a pained, disgusted look on her face.

"Her name's Mary," said Jackie, "I heard some of the others talking about her. A germ-a-phobe who's here to get over her fear of germs."

She and I both giggled a little about that. I didn't think she was off to a good start.

"And those two," Jackie continued, "are called Gil and Stark."

The men she referred two dropped their brush, which scared the horse and caused it to knock one of them over.

"The Apple Dumpling gang of the west," snickered Jackie. "I was watching them at breakfast. They're not too bright."

"How is it you seem to know everything?" I asked.

"I pay attention."

"Hey you two," said Joe, pointing at us, "Get to work. If you don't want to be here, then go somewhere else."

Frowning, Jackie went back to her horse.

I stared at mine unsure of what to do. Every time I reached out to stroke it with the brush, it snorted and moved.

"Come on you," I muttered, "I just want to brush you."

The horse snorted again and stepped forward; this time hitting my foot.

"You're scaring her," said a voice.

I looked up into the eyes of a man I hadn't remembered seeing on the grounds. "What?"

"You're moving too fast," said the man, "You need to be more gentle. Like this."

He took the brush from me. With practiced movements, he reached up and gently stroked the back of the horse in long strokes. While grooming the animal, the man talked soothingly to it.

"See? Like that. Now you try it."

I took the brush from him.

"There you go. Long, gentle strokes. And don't be afraid to talk to the animal."

I followed the man's directions. After a while, the horse seemed to have warmed up to me and remained still so that I could finish grooming it.

"Now you seem to be getting the hang of it," said the man.

"What's your name?" I asked.

"Jedidiah." The man tipped his big hat to me with a bit of straw clenched between his teeth.

"Good job," said Joe as he walked up. "You'd make a fair horse groomer."

"Thanks," I said.

Jedidiah had disappeared. I figured he just went to help someone else.

"Alright," said Joe, "Next we will learn how to saddle a horse and start riding."

A scream echoed around us. Mary's horse had pooped right on her foot causing her to run away in a panic. She shouted something about viruses and bacteria while she darted inside.

"That is so disgusting," said Liz as she watched the commotion.

Joe ran his fingers over his face in aggravation. I felt for him. "Poppy, the saddles."

Poppy came out with a saddle for each horse. The next twenty minutes were spent listening to Joe explain how to properly put a saddle on a horse and cinch it up. He explained every detail before letting us try. To my surprise, Aunt Ethel got hers on in the first go.

A scuffle drew my attention. Gil and Stark both lay face down in the mud with the saddle on top of both of them as their horse galloped away. Not too bright was right.

After another half hour of watching a bunch of inept city folk attempt to saddle a horse, Joe had had enough.

"City folk," he muttered to himself. "All right, everyone, that's it for today. Same time tomorrow if you're still interested. And assuming I don't drink myself into a stupor from all this nonsense."

I didn't think that last bit was meant to be heard. Most acted as though they hadn't understood a word out of his mouth anyway.

Everyone went their separate ways. Since lunchtime had rolled around, Jackie and I decided to head for the cafeteria/diner they had inside.

"Find us a table," I told Jackie, "I need to get a spare key for our room."

"Okay."

Jackie and I parted. I went to the front desk where the lady from the day before sat reading a travel magazine. "Hi," I said, "I need a spare key from room 206."

The woman put her magazine down sighing heavily. She walked to the mess of keys behind her and grabbed one. "Anything else?" she said as she handed me the key.

"No. Thank you."

A couple of voices caught my attention. I moved closer, hiding behind some shelves, not wanting to be noticed.

"I'm telling you his name was Michael Evans," said one. "He was here from Chicago."

"Do you know why?" asked the other.

"Probably to experience the Old West like everyone else who's here. The guy was a pawn broker going on about how he had found something important. Wouldn't stop talking about it."

"No wonder he got murdered."

"Yeah, well, pawn brokers aren't the most loved people anyway. And I hear that he was a bit of a shyster. Always conned people out of their precious items for way less than they were worth. Then, he'd sell them at a really marked up price."

"Maybe the killer did us a favor."

The other laughed. "Maybe."

The two men walked off continuing their conversation elsewhere. I headed for the cafeteria and found Jackie waiting for me at a table near a window.

"Where's Aunt Ethel?" I asked.

"She said something about having a prior engagement."

"Engagement? Like a date?"

"Not a pleasant thought is it? Hey, how'd you get so good at dealing with horses? You've never been around them your entire life."

"Some guy helped me," I said.

"Cute?"

"Jackie!"

"Well, was he?"

"Yeah, I suppose. Well, he was older, but not bad. But don't tell Greg."

"Oh, come on you're allowed to look," said Jackie with a smirk.

A bout of laughter interrupted our conversation.

"Rachel," I said, "We can't see you."

Rachel materialized beside us allowing us to see her, but not anyone else.

"What's so funny?" I asked.

"You," said Rachel. "You thought that guy was good looking."

"Why is that so funny?"

"Because he's a ghost," Rachel blurted out. "You thought a ghost was cute!" She started another round of laughter shaking the entire table. All anyone else saw was a table moving by itself.

Jackie and I grabbed hold of it attempting to stop its rocking motion.

"Uneven legs," I smiled at a couple that passed by. "Rachel, stop it. You're drawing people's attention!"

"Really? I'll show you how to attract attention."

Rachel took my wallet from my purse and walked over to the salad bar. She picked up two premade salads and went to the cashier. "How much?"

"The lady at the cashier didn't even look up. "$8.50."

"Here you go." Rachel handed her a ten dollar bill and accepted the change.

Only then did the cashier look up. She did a double take as the salads and my wallet floated across the room to where Jackie and I sat.

"Bon apetit!" Rachel placed the tray in front of us.

Jackie and I opened our salads while I scanned the area hoping no one watched us. I thought I saw Poppy looking at me, but he jerked away the moment I turned in his direction. Strange fellow, I thought.

"Salt?" asked Jackie.

Rachel reached over and snatched a salt shaker from someone's hand before handing it to Jackie. The poor guy just that there with a perplexed look on his face trying to figure what just happened.

"You'll never guess what I found out about the dead guy in our room," I said leaning close to Jackie.

"Oh?"

"Two guys were talking about him in the lobby. Apparently he was a pawn broker from Chicago going on about discovering something big—something that meant a lot of money."

"What did he discover?" asked Jackie.

"They didn't know. But I'm willing to bet that that was why he was killed."

"Well, this time we should let the cops handle it," said Jackie. "You remember what Detective Shorts said. And he can't bail you out this time. Why don't we forget about the murder and actually enjoy ourselves for once."

"Yeah, you're right," I reluctantly agreed. After all, I didn't have my usual friends here to help me.

"Oh, there you are, darling," said Aunt Ethel as she sat next to us. "I'm glad you two got started already. I was a little busy. Anyway, I heard there is a great antique shop in town. We should all go there this afternoon."

Jackie and I both groaned. Neither of us liked antiquing, but it was Aunt Ethel's favorite pastime. Knowing there was no getting out of it, we agreed.

"Perfect!" Aunt Ethel picked up her bag. "I'll see you both after lunch and don't be late."

"Don't be late she says," muttered Jackie. "Maybe we should just not show up."

I glared at her.

"What? She never said anything about making sure we were there."

"It's sort of implied."

We took my car to town, which was about twenty miles away. Aunt Ethel sat in the back with pursed lips. She did not approve of the paint job on my car.

"I do hope that you plan to get this repainted," she said.

"Yes, Aunt Ethel," I replied.

The thirty minute car ride consisted of Jackie and I listening to Aunt Ethel drone on about various antiques and how they would make a nice addition to her home. Relief flooded over me when we finally pulled into the one-street town. I park in the nearest available space.

"Aunt Ethel," I said, "Jackie and I thought we would look around at some of the other shops. We don't really feel like antiquing."

"Well, all right, dear," said Aunt Ethel with slight disappointment. "Stay out of trouble."

"Will do."

I waved Jackie onward. We cruised the various tables set up with all sorts of things for tourists to spend money on. Some claimed to have real Indian artifacts. Others had homemade quilts and recipe books with the sort of recipes used by the pioneers.

I walked past all of them. Their stuff looked nice; I just didn't feel like spending money. Besides, my suitcase only held so much and I wasn't going to load my car up with stuff I didn't need.

Someone grabbed my arm and yanked me aside. "Hey!"

"Shush," said Rachel. "So, what's the plan?"

"Plan?"

"Yeah. For finding the killer." Rachel gave me an expectant look.

"This time I thought I'd let the cops handle it."

Rachel placed her hands on her hips. "Oh, so Mel no longer wants to solve mysteries."

"It's not that," I said, "It's just it might be best if I didn't get involved."

"Considering the dead guy was found in your room, I'd say you're already involved. Come on. Jedidiah said that that Michael Evans was snooping around for the last week."

"Jedidiah?" said Jackie.

"Yeah. He's inside waiting for us. Said that that Michael came here a lot. Come on."

"Who's Jedidiah?" asked Jackie.

It turned out that Jedidiah was the ghost that instructed me on how to properly groom a horse. The same ghost that I thought was good looking for a man in his forties. Oh yeah, I know how to pick them.

Next thing I knew, Rachel pulled me and Jackie into a bar. A bunch of people in cowboy hats sat around laughing and drinking while playing pool. I never felt more out of place.

"Well, howdy!"

Jedidiah tipped his hat toward me. Only Jackie and I could see him. "Nice seeing you again."

"We should find a table and order some drinks before people start to think we're weird," said Jackie.

I glanced around the room and realized she was right so I walked over to the bar itself. "Two beers," I said hoping it was an innocuous enough drink.

This place didn't strike me as the sort of establishment that sold those fancy fruity drinks. The man behind the counter plopped two bottles of Budweiser in front of us.

I thought I felt eyes upon me. I glanced around and found Poppy sitting in a far corner staring at Jackie and I. "What's he doing here?"

"What?" said Jackie.

"Poppy. The handyman from the ranch. He's over there."

"He's probably just here to get a drink like everyone else," replied Jackie. "This is the only bar in town."

"Go on," urged Rachel, "Ask that fella what Michael Evans wanted when he came here."

"Why don't you ask him," I said. "Rachel, this isn't a good idea. I think we ought to leave."

"You know, people are starting to stare at you," said Jedidiah, "They must think you're a bit crazy talking to ghosts and all."

"Probably because they can't see the ghosts," I mumbled as I placed my head in my hands. "Let's go, Jackie."

Jackie looked relieved as she placed her half drunk beer back on the counter.

"Bar is closed," said a big man in a Stetson.

Great, the one thing I wanted to avoid. "We we're just leaving."

"You know, I'm tired of you tourists coming in here and dropping your money as though you're better than all of us."

The guy was starting to get on my nerves. "Look," I said, "We're leaving. Just get out of our way."

"Oh, where are my manners? Excuse me." The guy stepped aside with a mock curtsey; much to the laughter of his friends.

Jackie and I started for the door.

"You're not going to take this from him are you?" said Rachel.

"Let it go, Rachel," I hissed out the side of my mouth.

"After all," said the man, "We don't need some nutcase who talks to herself in our town. Go back to the nuthouse you escaped from."

"That's it," said Rachel, rolling up her sleeves, "No one talks to my friend that way."

She charged the guy and jumped onto his back bringing him to the floor head first. Every one watched as the guy reeled backward from a series of invisible punches.

"Take that you no good—" Rachel continued to lay into the man. A chair seemed to hover in midair as she smashed it on top of the man's head.

"She attacked him," yelled another.

He and his buddies started for Jackie and I. Rachel shoved a table in front of them tripping them. The next thing I knew, the entire place erupted into one huge brawl. Bottles, chairs, and glasses flew everywhere as people attacked one another. Jackie and I darted behind the counter just as a couple of beer bottles came our way.

"Wee doggie," yelled Jedidiah, "I hadn't been in a fight like this for a hundred and thirty years!" He charged into the fray tackling some guy.

The man that had hassled me landed on the floor beside me. "You!"

I snatched a bottle and bashed him over the head with it.

"Yay! Way to go, Mel," shouted Rachel. She kicked someone in the gut.

"YEE-HAW!" Jedidiah swung on one of the lights sailing over the fighting mass of people until he rammed into a man standing on the bar counter. The guy tumbled over and into the mirror directly behind him.

"Ow!" Jackie held her hand over her eye after receiving a punch.

"That's my friend you jerk!" Rachel crashed into the

man that had punched Jackie at the same time I did. To-gether we held him down while Jackie landed in a few kicks.

"I never knew you had violent tendencies," I joked to Jackie.

"The way I figure it, he deserved it and we're probably going to get arrested for this; so might as well make it worth it." Jackie picked up a stool and hit someone in the back with it.

"Behind you, Mel!"

I turned around just in time to dodge someone's fist. I punched the man in the chin and gave another hit to his stomach.

"Wooo-hoo," yelled Jedidiah, "Nothing like a friend-ly brawl to make you feel alive." He threw a bulky man across the room.

BOOM! BOOM!

The two gun shots startled everyone to a complete halt. Bruised and bloodied people looked up to see what had interrupted their fun.

In the bar entrance stood Sheriff Judson and his dep-uties. One of them held a smoking shot gun that he had just fired twice to get our attention. All motion stopped.

"All right," yelled Sheriff Judson, "What goes on here?"

"They started it!" Everyone pointed fingers at Jackie and I. How original.

"Okay, girls," said the Sheriff. "I got to take you in." He had one of his deputies escort Jackie and I to the jail. "The rest of you remain put. You'll be staying here until I can get to the bottom of this."

"Now wait a minute, Sheriff," said the man that had accosted Jackie and I.

"Earl," said Sheriff Judson, "I'll take you in too. Now sit your butt down."

The man did as ordered.

"All right, Charlie, take them in," said the sheriff, "I'll be there in a bit."

Jackie and I allowed ourselves to be led away; not like we had much choice. Within fifteen minutes we were processed and sitting in a jail cell. The only jail cell in the Sheriff's office.

Rachel and Jedidiah sat in the cell with us wearing more somber expressions than Jackie and I. I'm not sure why they decided to lock themselves up. It's not as though the deputy saw them, nor could a ghost be tried in a court of law. Though I would love to have seen such a thing. Could you imagine any judge putting Rachel on trial?

I'm not sure how much time passed, but Jackie and I waited until the sun had set before the sheriff walked in with Aunt Ethel. The expression on her face said it all. Aunt Ethel was livid.

"Mellow darling, I'm surprised at you," scolded Aunt Ethel, "The pair of you getting into a bar fight. What would your mothers think?"

Nothing, if you don't say anything.

"I know you girls were raised better than this." Aunt Ethel turned to the Sheriff who watched the exchange with mild interest. "Sherriff Judson, how much is the bail for both of them?" She dug into her purse for her wallet.

"Nothing," answered the sheriff.

"I beg your pardon," said Aunt Ethel.

"The owner of the bar refuses to press charges," said Sheriff Judson, "He admits that they didn't start the fight. In fact, I have a surveillance tape that shows Earl getting attacked by thin air. Your girls were simply in the wrong place at the wrong time.

"So, I'm letting them go. But stay out of the bar in the future."

Jackie and I gladly left the cell once the door opened.

"I do appreciate this," said Aunt Ethel.

I noticed the drawers in the sheriff's desk open on their own as Rachel rifled through them.

"No problem," said the Sheriff. "Earl is kind of the laughing stock of the town right the moment."

A cabinet opened and closed.

"But, uh," continued Sheriff Judson, "I mean it about staying away from the bar."

"Of course they will." Aunt Ethel shuffled us out of the sheriff's office.

The exit opened by itself as Jedidiah held it for us. "Ma'am," he said tipping his hat.

Aunt Ethel did a slight double take before glancing at me. I shrugged my shoulders in a "let it go" way.

"Really, Mellow, getting into a drunken brawl," said Aunt Ethel as she continued to lecture me.

"Rachel started it," I said.

"Yes, I did," bragged Rachel.

"Get in the car," ordered my aunt as she opened the door to the driver's seat.

Suddenly, the car door slammed shut causing Aunt

Ethel to jump back. "You and driving don't go well to-gether," said Rachel to my aunt, "In the back seat."

"Well. I never," huffed my aunt as she crawled into the back seat.

Rachel opened the door for me. "Your chariot awaits."

"You know, you really shouldn't get her riled up like that."

Rachel chuckled devilishly as she climbed into the rear with Jedidiah and my aunt.

"I don't think I've ever been in one of these," said Jedidiah, "Moves all by itself."

Dreading the drive back to the ranch, I started the car and pulled onto the road with four passengers: two of whom were living, the other two were ghosts.

CHAPTER 4

"And furthermore, Mellow dear," my Aunt Ethel continued her lecture as we walked into her room.

"Enough, Aunt Ethel," I blurted out, my anger getting the best of me. "For the last forty minutes you have done nothing but lecture me about the evil of my ways. I've had it! Either shut up, or Jackie and I will leave right now."

A series of claps sounded around us as Rachel jumped up and down. "Oh," she said when she noticed the displeased looks on both my face and Aunt Ethel's.

"Well, I never," said Aunt Ethel.

"Well, the young lady here has a point," added Jedidiah.

"Uh, what's this?" asked Jackie as she pulled an ornate box out of a bag.

"That," said Aunt Ethel grabbing the box, "Is a cigar box. It's an antique dating back to the pioneer days."

Jackie took the box from my aunt and examined it. "It says 'made in Japan' on the bottom."

"What!" Aunt Ethel snatched the cigar box and read the small inscription on the bottom. She let her hand fall not wanting to believe that she had been conned.

I took the object from her. Sure enough, it had been made in Japan.

"Ha-ha! You just got Shanghaied," laughed Jedidiah. "Happens all the time. Ain't anyone I know who ever carried something that fancy out here."

"How much did you pay for that?" asked Jackie.

"About three hundred dollars," answered Aunt Ethel.

My fingers felt something loosen. Curious, I pulled at it until the bottom popped off. Out fell a piece of paper all torn and smudged. I put the box down and carefully unfolded the paper so as to not tear it any more than it already was. It looked very old. "It's a map."

Jackie reached for it. I handed it to her so she could study it. "It certainly does look like a map. That box had a false bottom in it."

"Probably fake," said Jedidiah.

"I don't think so," I said taking the map back, "It looks genuine. The box may have been fake, but this looks real enough. Is there anyone in town who might know more about these things?"

All anger gone from earlier, Aunt Ethel jumped at the chance of learning about the map. "I heard about a woman who's somewhat of a local historian. Shouldn't be too hard to find her."

"I'll go ask around," I said, folding up the map. I put it in my pocket determined to keep it near me. "I think we ought to go to bed. In the morning we can get this sorted out."

"Very well," said Aunt Ethel, "And don't lose that."

Jackie and I went back to our room. Rachel and Jedidiah had disappeared, which didn't surprise me.

We set out early the next morning in search of the local historian. Sal had given me directions. We spent a good hour in the car driving along a seemingly abandoned dirt road before coming upon a house in the middle of nowhere.

"I hope she likes visitors," whispered Jackie.

I thought the same thing. One could literally disappear out here. We exited the car and headed for the front door; Aunt Ethel in the lead.

"Yes," said a middle aged woman as she answered the door.

"Some people in town said that you are a local historian of sorts," I said, "We found this old map and wanted to know if it's authentic."

The woman opened the door allowing us inside.

"My name is Mel and this is Jackie and my Aunt Ethel," I said introducing us.

"Louise. Won't you sit down?"

We helped ourselves to a few chairs in her living room. She had a nice looking place with modest decorations, family and farming pictures on the wall, and a fireplace. An old wood stove sat in the corner of the room.

"This is what we found in a cigar box that my aunt

bought thinking it was a real antique." I handed Louise the map and the box.

She took them both and examined them. "I recognize this sort of box," she said, "People back in the twenties and thirties used to buy everyday objects, age them, and then sell them as pioneer things. This sort of thing still goes on today. Many a tourist has been tricked into buying something they thought dated back to the 1850s or something."

My aunt pursed her lips clearly steamed about being tricked.

"Now this map is something else." Louise held it up to the light. She fumbled through a drawer for a magnifying glass. I looked around some more as we waited for her to finish her examination. It didn't take her long.

"It looks authentic enough," she said, "This paper definitely seems to be of the type used back in the 1800s. The ink is a bit faded like it should be, but in fairly good condition. What interests me is what it is."

"What is it?" asked Aunt Ethel.

"If I'm right, this could be map for the treasure of Josiah Bard. He was a known outlaw in these parts back in 1888. Supposedly, he robbed banks and stagecoaches that passed through here. But when the law found him, he had nothing. He said he put his treasure where none but the foolish would find it.

"Many people have been through here looking for his lost treasure, but they've all come up empty. Some have even died looking for it. Of course, none of them had a map."

"Is it real?" I asked.

"Well, the pen strokes match what was used back

then," said Louise, "And the paper seems to be from the same era. Carbon dating could tell you for sure. Also, right here where it's a bit faded you can see Josiah's name." She pointed to a corner of the map. With the magnifying glass I was able to make out Josiah Bard's name.

"Interesting thing is," continued Louise," you aren't the first ones to bring me this map."

"We aren't?" I asked.

"About a week ago some fella from Chicago came here with a map just like this. Except it was an obvious copy from the 1930s. The paper and ink gave it away. Then yesterday, two other fellas came by here with the same exact map. And I mean the same exact one. All of them interested if it really was a map to Josiah Bard's riches.

"And now here you are with the same map, except this one looks more like the original."

"Do you remember the other two men's names?" Jackie asked.

"No, but they weren't the brightest in the bunch. Kept knocking things over or just getting all mixed up."

That sounded like Gil and Stark. Could they have heard about the treasure and killed Michael Evans for the map? It was possible.

"Now, I'm going to tell you the same thing I told the others," said Louise, "Stay out of this. Real or not, Josiah's lost treasure has brought nothing but trouble to any who went looking for it. A lot of folk have gone missing in the Badlands because they went hunting for it and got lost.

"Josiah's money went missing long ago. If he did bury it in these hills, he meant for it to stay there."

Figuring it was time to leave, I stood up. "Thank you for your time."

"Don't thank me. Always like helping folks," said Louise, "But I mean it. Don't go looking for it. Real or not, you'll most likely become food for the wild critters around here if you go searching."

We each thanked Louise before piling into my car.

"A real live treasure hunt," beamed Aunt Ethel as I pulled back onto the road. "Just think. The excitement!"

"Weren't we just warned to not go looking for it?" asked Jackie.

"But we have a real treasure map. Josiah Bard's map," said Aunt Ethel.

"You didn't even know who he was until now," retorted Jackie.

"Doesn't matter," said Aunt Ethel. "We have an opportunity to have an adventure and I'm not going to miss it for the world."

"Shoot!" I blurted out.

"What is it, dear?" asked Aunt Ethel.

"I need to email project updates to my professor," I replied, "You two don't mind if we make a quick stop in town do you?"

"No," said Jackie, "Besides we can get some lunch there."

CHAPTER 5

I parked the car in the center of the town when we arrived. The town was so small, I figured that this was the easiest thing to do. I told Jackie and Aunt Ethel that I would meet them at the local diner.

The library wasn't hard to find nor was it that big. The librarian gave me a passcode to use when logging onto the computer. As I waited for the thing to log onto the web, I tried to think of what I could say to my professor. I hadn't exactly worked on my project at all since I arrived.

I glanced at the computer and realized that I'd be waiting for a while. Dial up was so slow. How did we ever survive without a high speed connection?

I wandered over to the window while I waited. Movement caught my eye. Gil and Stark walked briskly from the hardware store with a wrapped bundle. Stark tripped. They both fell to the ground with their bundle flying open spilling various tools everywhere. Gil looked up and saw me watching. Instantly, he jumped to his feet and began gathering up the tools. Together, they managed to get everything and ran off.

I started to head for the door so I could follow them, but the computer beeped indicating it had finally connected to the web. Grudgingly, I went to the monitor and brought up my email. After a few sentences that stretched the truth, by a lot, I sent my message off. Hopefully it would buy me some time before I had to submit anything substantial.

I walked out into the brisk afternoon sun. You'd think that in March the weather would start warming up. Not in this area. A few snow patches informed me that we weren't that far out of winter.

I found the diner and spotted Jackie and Aunt Ethel immediately. The only waitress in this place appeared to be a plump, black woman with her hair pulled tightly back. I guess they didn't get much business in a place this size.

Jackie and Aunt Ethel had already started eating. They each had sandwiches with fries, which surprised me.

Aunt Ethel never ate fries. "They make me gassy," she had informed me once.

This will make for an interesting car ride back to the ranch, I thought.

"What'll you have?" asked the waitress.

I realized that I hadn't even looked at the menu. I spotted a white board that had that day's special written on it: turkey sandwich with coleslaw. "The special, please," I said.

"Anything to drink?"

"Water's fine."

"Do you have any soup?" I asked suddenly, wanting something a bit warm.

"Chicken noodle. The finest chicken noodle soup in the west," beamed the waitress.

"A bowl of that too. Thanks."

"Coming right up." The waitress flipped her notepad closed.

"Hey, beautiful," said a man I didn't recognize. "My name is Calhoun. I'm sure you've noticed me at the ranch."

"Nope. Can't say that I have," I said, hoping he'd leave. Though to be honest, I didn't remember seeing him at the ranch.

"Oh sure you have," Calhoun took a seat next to me.

The waitress walked up with my bowl of soup and placed it in front of me.

Calhoun took the soup away from me and started eating it. "I'm a lawyer from Las Vegas. I know you know who I am."

The word, jerk, floated through my mind.

"Anyway, we ought to get together," continued Calhoun.

"Look, pal, I don't care who you are and that is my soup you're eating." Anger rose within me.

"I'm doing you a favor," snorted Calhoun, "This stuff is horrible."

"Young man," said Aunt Ethel, her cheeks turning red, "You were not invited to this table. My niece is hardly interested in trash, such as yourself, now leave."

"Now, listen here, you warthog," said Calhoun. "I'll go when I'm good and ready—OW!"

Aunt Ethel had rammed one of the heels of her shoes into the man's foot.

"Why I ought to—"

"Want me to shove his face into that soup?" asked the waitress.

"You can't do that," said Calhoun.

In answer to his outburst, the waitress reached out and pushed his face right into the bowl of soup. He gurgled as some of it went down his windpipe.

"I'll have your job for this," shouted Calhoun, soup dripping onto his shirt.

"Hold on," said the waitress, "I'll get you the owner." She turned in a circle and looked straight into his eyes. "What do you want?"

"You're the owner?" said a stunned Calhoun.

"Yeah," said the woman, "And that'll be twenty bucks for the soup."

"For soup? It doesn't cost that much."

"It does when I don't like you."

"I'm not paying."

"Hey, Rusty!" shouted the waitress, "Some boob here don't like your cooking."

A lid clanged on a pot. Two local guys at the counter scrambled out of the diner. The door to the kitchen opened up and there stood eight feet of pure tattooed muscle with a stained apron.

"Who no like my cooking?" said the man in a thick Russian accent. He walked over to our table and stared down at Calhoun. "You not like my cooking?"

A series of unrecognizable syllables spilled out of Calhoun's mouth.

"He also owes me twenty bucks," said the waitress.
"Now I'm not—"

Rusty picked the man up as though he weighed nothing.

"Here." Calhoun held out his wallet.

The cook took it, pulled out a twenty, and handed it back to the man. "Now get out. And don't come back."

Calhoun ran out of the building tripping over a chair.

"I'll get you a new bowl," the waitress took the soup that Calhoun had helped himself to, "Seeing as how it's contaminated and all."

"Remind me to never anger anyone in this place," said Jackie when we were alone.

The waitress came back with my order. "Enjoy."

After she had left, the salt shaker moved on its own as the top of my sandwich lifted up. I watched as my lunch salted itself. "Rachel," I said.

"Just trying to help," said Rachel s she put the salt down. "Oh, and Jedidiah says that if you all are interested in that treasure hunt, make sure you join that Old West Trail Ride tomorrow. It leaves at dawn. And pack some warm things and plenty of food and water."

"We never said we were—"

"Of course we're going," interrupted Aunt Ethel. "I'm not getting any younger and have always wanted to go on a treasure hunt."

"Tell Jedidiah we'll be ready," I told Rachel.

We ate the rest of our meal in silence. Afterward, we headed to the local grocer and bought what canned and dried food and bottled water there was. A part of me kept thinking that it was obvious we were planning a hiking trip. I just hoped that whomever had murdered Michael Evans didn't find out about it.

By evening, we arrived back at the ranch. As I hauled our purchases inside, I bumped into Liz, or Miss Hollywood as I dubbed her.

"Watch where you're going," she scolded me. "You made me chip a nail."

"Who cares," I blurted out. I didn't mean to; it just slipped out.

Liz gave me a nasty look before continuing on her way.

"So, how did your aunt pick this place again?" asked Jackie as she walked up beside me.

"Google told her it would be a great place to 'get away from it all'."

"I'll be up in a moment, dear," said Aunt Ethel, "I need to talk to the front desk. My room was a bit drafty last night and I got a terrible chill."

"That might be because I opened the window," said Rachel when my aunt left.

I gave her a look.

"What?" said Rachel, "I didn't want her to suffocate. Just trying to be nice. Here I got that." She took one of the bags from me and carried it up the steps.

I scanned the room hoping that no one saw the floating bag. Quickly, Jackie and I raced up the stairs. Just as we got halfway to our room, Mary came out of hers. She saw the floating bags of stuff and stopped cold.

"What? Like you never saw a bag of groceries move on its own before," said Rachel as she walked past.

A panicked expression washed over Mary's face. She

rushed back to her room. After wiping the door handle with a sanitary wipe, she bolted inside and shut the door.

Just then Calhoun stepped out of his room. "I just want you to know that I am suing you," he said to me.

"Over my dead body," snapped Rachel.

Calhoun glanced at the floating bags of canned goods. Confused, he just stared at them. It suddenly dropped landing right on his foot.

"That's assault!" he shouted. "Hey, you," he waved at Poppy who had appeared from nowhere, "You saw what happened."

"I ain't seen nothing," said Poppy.

"I'll sue this whole establishment."

Calhoun turned to go back into his room. The door slammed in his face with the distinctive click of the lock turning. He jiggled the door handle. Nothing happened.

"I had a key here someplace," said Calhoun as he searched his pockets.

"He mean this key?" laughed Jedidiah as he held up a key.

"Jedidiah," snickered Rachel, "I'm starting to like you. Come on." She picked up the bags of groceries and we all headed to our room.

"Hey, you, get this door open," said Calhoun to Poppy.

Poppy sighed heavily and headed for the stairs mumbling something about needing to get his tools.

"Hey, I'm not through with you," Calhoun said to me.

"Shut up." Jedidiah shoved him into the wall. Of course, all Calhoun saw was thin air.

"I really don't like that guy," said Jackie once we were

in our room. "Hot shot lawyer from Las Vegas thinks he can run everything."

"What time are we leaving tomorrow?" I asked.

"Dawn, dear," said Aunt Ethel as she entered the room. "I just need to find us a guide."

"You got one right here," said Jedidiah as he materialized. "I know this place quite well. Used to do a lot of trading and trapping in this area. That was after I failed at striking it rich during the gold rush in California."

"Then it's settled," said Aunt Ethel. "Now we need tools. The lady at the desk helped me make a list."

"Got that too," said Jedidiah as he took the list from my aunt. "Don't worry. I'll get everything you need."

"Very well. I guess it's time we eat and go to bed." Aunt Ethel left the room.

"You know," whispered Jackie to me, "Your aunt is taking this ghost thing quite well."

"Yeah, an encounter with Rachel will do that to you," I replied.

CHAPTER 6

Morning arrived rather quickly. I felt like I had just fallen asleep when Jackie shook me awake.

"Rise and shine," she chirruped. "It's time to get up and find us some treasure. Let's have an adventure."

I gaped at her and her unusual peppiness. "You know, Jackie, I don't think it's going to be as glorious as it sounds. Remember, Michael Evans was probably killed for that map and the killer probably wants the treasure as well."

"Well, you certainly know how to put a damper on things."

"Giddy up, ya'll!" Rachel appeared in our room dressed like she was part of some sort of rodeo. "You really need to learn how to be a morning person," she said to me.

"Says the girl who doesn't need to sleep." I crawled out of bed and got dressed.

"So how's our not so nice friend?" asked Jackie.

"He ended up sleeping in the lobby," replied Rachel, "For some strange reason, no matter how hard they tried they couldn't get his door open.

"Oh, and Joe is complaining about someone stealing tools from the shed. And the two bumbling idiots (Gil and Stark) left sometime last night. Joe isn't happy about that either. They took a couple of horses and he's complaining about having to send a search party for them if they don't return.

"Anyway, best hurry. Everyone is waiting by the barn."

Aunt Ethel waved us over when Jackie and I appeared outside. "Jedidiah said to take these horses."

I looked through the saddle bags noting that the food we had bought were there along with some tools: shovel, pick, and some other stuff.

"I think I know where the missing tools went," I muttered to Jackie.

"Alright, ladies and gentlemen," said Joe, "On your horses. It will take about two hours to get to the town. Once there you can wander as you like and we will return here by sundown."

"Uh, I need some air freshener or something because this animal reeks," said Liz, in her designer workout clothes.

"Oh, Jesus and Mary above help me," muttered Joe as he rubbed his hands over his face.

I watched as Mary tried to get on her horse without touching it. Even Calhoun joined our group, much to my displeasure.

The cloudy morning brought a chill that practically froze my hands. Good thing I had brought an extra pair of gloves.

The group was mostly quiet as we rode, except... "This saddle. is chafing. my new workout pants. They'll be. ruined by the end of the day. I spent three hundred dollars on workout pants and they won' even last a week at this rate!" Liz kept whining with every jostle from her horse. Mary put hand sanitizer on her hands every few minutes. No one noticed the two horses with empty saddles trailing behind.

Calhoun kept giving me dirty looks. Rachel flung a rock at him. He looked all around for the culprit, but found nothing. How do you accuse a ghost of harassing you?

The sky was starting to cloud up when we arrived at the Old West town two hours later. He explained that it was built by the ranch owner so that guests could get an idea of what life was like back then. People dressed in pioneer clothes moved about doing their chores; actors hired for the moment, but it did bring a sort of reality to it.

"Feel free to wander around," said Joe, "There's stores and a saloon. Have yourselves a good time."

Aunt Ethel, Jackie, and I dismounted our horses.

Jedidiah took the reins. "Meet me by the General Store in an hour," he said.

"Oh look," said Aunt Ethel, "A clothing shop." She went in.

"Get your hands up," said Rachel pointing a fake gun at me. "You stole my cattle. Now you gonna pay." Click! She pulled the trigger of her cap gun and laughed hysterically.

"I think you're having a little too much fun," I said.

"And you're not having enough," said Rachel. "Let's check out the saloon."

"No," I said, "remember the last time we entered a bar? Come on. Let's grab Aunt Ethel and meet Jedidiah."

Just then, Aunt Ethel walked out with a coat made almost entirely of feathers. "Isn't it wonderful? The lady in there said that a real Indian Chief wore this. Should keep me nice and warm on our trip."

"Meet your Aunt Ethel," whispered Jackie, "The most gullible tourist with money."

We found Jedidiah who waited patiently. "Ready?"

Yeah," I said.

"Then let's go before anyone notices us."

Each of us mounted a horse and galloped off with Jedidiah in the lead. No one paid any attention to us.

CHAPTER 7

Small snowflakes marked the beginning of our journey through the South Dakota wilderness. Jedidiah told me that we were not far from the North Dakota border. Of course to him the entire territory was Dakota Territory. The gray sky loomed over us and the temperature dropped a few degrees as we made our way northward to the Badlands.

To anyone who might have happened to observe us, we would look like three women with five horses. Though we could see Jedidiah and Rachel, no one else would have. Ghosts tend to decide who sees them and who doesn't. However, if you do not believe in such things then you will see nothing.

Aunt Ethel and Rachel passed the time singing some

drinking song. The fact that my Aunt Ethel joined in amazed me. Or that she even knew a drinking song.

"Damn," said Jackie, "There really are such things as dead zones."

"Please tell me you did not bring your cell phone," I said to her.

"Because you never know when you might need to call someone," said Jackie. A sheepish expression crossed her face when she said it. Jackie put her phone back in her pocket and snapped the reins of her horse.

"Oh, I wish I were a pirate," sang Rachel.

I gaped at her. "Pirate?"

"Wrong kind of song?" asked Rachel with an innocent expression. "We might as well be pirates since we are looking for buried treasure. But I guess we could sing *Home on the Range.*"

"No thank you," I said.

Most of the afternoon passed uneventfully as we rode through the wilderness. Snow flurries continued to plague us threatening to turn into a storm.

"Even in March, it has been known to blizzard," said Jedidiah when I had voiced my concern about the snow.

I cinched my coat even tighter. I hoped this treasure would be worth it.

"But think of the glory that lies ahead," said Aunt Ethel.

Leave it to my aunt to try and make an adventure out of something.

We rode until dark, which happened quickly with all of the cloud cover. Jedidiah had us stop near some lonely brush to which we tied our horses. He instructed Jackie on how to build a fire. It wasn't big, but provided some warmth. Jackie also grabbed the kettle and one of the many cans of beans we had.

"Well if this doesn't clean out my system, I don't know what will," said Aunt Ethel as she chowed down on her serving of beans.

That statement made me lose my appetite a bit. Of all the things to say when people are trying to eat.

Rachel stared at my bowl of beans. "You know, there are times when I am glad that I don't have to eat."

"You're welcome to it," I said.

"No. No, you need your strength."

I fiddled with my beans at first, but eventually resigned myself to eating them. I couldn't very well go hungry on the entire trip.

"How far are we from the Badlands?" I asked.

"Not far at all," said Jedidiah. "Well you all better get some shut eye. And I suggest you stay near the fire. It's bound to get a might chilly."

A few snowflakes settled on my nose after he said that.

The next morning dawned with about an inch of snow on the ground. I shook it off of my sleeping bag just as Jackie and Aunt Ethel sat up.

"Oh my," said Aunt Ethel, "I do believe that it snowed last night."

"Never would have figured that one out," muttered Jackie.

"Everybody up," said Jedidiah.

I stood up and rolled my sleeping bag. After that, I doused the smoldering coals of the fire, which had mostly been put out by the snow anyway. I looked up at the still cloudy sky rubbing my chilled hands together. It had stopped snowing for the moment, but threatened more.

Skipping breakfast, we decided to get a move on. Within twenty minutes we had everything packed and rode off. Jedidiah kept talking about his days as a living person exploring this area. I tuned most of it out as the gray clouds stole most of my attention.

"Whoa!" Jackie's exclamation pulled me from my thoughts. Before us, stretched this huge expanse of canyons and ravines. Though not as big as the Grand Canyon, the Badlands was sizeable. From where I sat, it looked to be a vast maze of various ravines that twisted and wound around itself.

"Welcome to the Badlands," said Jedidiah. "There's a trail near here that will take us down in."

The sound of a gunshot echoed across the plains as a poof of dust rose up near my horse.

"Was that a gun shot?" asked Jackie.

In answer to her question another bullet hit nearby us. Whoever it was either was too far away to hit us, or meant to only scare us away.

"Long range rifle," said Jedidiah. "Probably with a scope."

Another shot rang out.

"Let's move!" Jedidiah kicked his horse and sped up with Jackie and Rachel close behind.

"How dare you fire at us you miscreant!" screamed Aunt Ethel.

"This isn't the time for that," I said to her as I smacked her horse's behind and together we chased after the others.

Hooves pounded the earth as each breath our horses took made small vapor clouds before us. I prayed that we wouldn't slip on any ice or step in any prairie dog holes.

Mirroring Jedidiah, I held on tightly to the reins and leaned forward slightly as I allowed my horse to move freely. A quick glance at my aunt told me she was not having a good time. She bobbed up and down on her horse like a ragdoll with one hand holding onto her outlandish hat and another clinging to the horse.

"This way!"

Jedidiah steered to the right going into the canyon itself. We followed him down the trail pushing our mounts hard as we escaped whomever had taken pot shots at us. As the trail narrowed and turned uneven, our guide slowed down and halted us. We remained still as we glanced behind making sure no one pursued us.

"I think we lost him," said Jedidiah. "Does anyone else know you have the map?"

"No," I said. "The only ones who would, would be those we asked about it."

"Well, someone knows you've got it," said Jedidiah.

"Let me at him!" yelled Rachel. "I'll kick him from here to the moon."

Jackie ended up having to hang onto Rachel's shirt to hold her back as she tried to run off. How that was possible is still beyond me, but it made for a very comical scene.

"Rachel," I said. "Now isn't the time. We should concentrate on finding the treasure first."

Rachel huffed a bit, but settled down. "Well, he just better hope I do not get my hands on him."

After we managed to get Rachel to calm down, Jedidiah led us into one of the many canyons that make up the Badlands. We ended up walking our horses the remainder of the way down.

The snow on the path made it slippery and many times one of us lost our balance and slid a bit. My horse snorted in my ear as my foot stepped on some loose pebbles and shot out from under me.

"Are you alright, dear," asked Aunt Ethel.

Nursing my sore butt, I nodded. "I'll be ok. Just my pride's hurt."

By midmorning we reached the bottom of the trail and continued eastward like the map had said. I had no idea how far we were to go. Some of the writing on it was faded a bit and I had to use a magnifying glass to read it. In the end, we decided to just keep going until we found a good spot to camp for the night.

Rolling thunder caught my attention. I looked behind us and noticed a buildup of clouds. An ominous feeling washed over me. Lightning flashed and more thunder reached my ears. By the magnitude of it, I could tell that it moved closer. I glanced around at the snow around us and at the canyon walls. As a sinking feeling came over me, I slowly realized that we were in a flood zone.

"What is it" asked Jackie when she noticed that I had stopped walking.

"Jedidiah," I called pointing out the cloud buildup. "Is that what I think it is?"

Jedidiah's brow furrowed as he studied the western sky. "We need to find high ground! Now!"

Thunder roared overhead as lightning lit up the sky. Jedidiah smacked the behind of his horse sending it running off. He urged us to do the same with our mounts.

More lightning. Rain fell from the sky as it opened up drenching us within moments. Instantly, the snow around us melted as puddles formed.

We ran for higher ground struggling to climb upward as the dirt turned into slick mud. I looked back. Aunt Ethel struggled to hold her horse which had panicked from the sudden storm.

"Leave him!" yelled Jedidiah. "The horses will take care of themselves." He ran to my aunt and lifted her up. I watched as she seemingly kicked and screamed at thin air while floating over to where the rest of us attempted to climb higher. He placed Aunt Ethel on a ledge and heaved her upward.

The ground rumbled as a roar filled my ears. It built in intensity until it reached a deafening pitch. "What's that?" I asked.

We all glanced to our right as a wall of water headed straight for us. I said headed. More like it charged for us in an attempt to seize us before we had a chance to escape.

"Keep climbing!" shouted Jedidiah at us.

We wasted no time climbing. Rachel and Jedidiah helped Aunt Ethel who struggled against the slippery earth.

My foot slipped in the mud. Instantly, I lunged for a protruding rock. As though to add insult to injury, the rock popped out of the earth and I fell to the raging water below.

"Mel!"

A thousand needles stabbed me as I hit the water being instantly carted away. I poked my head through the surface taking a deep breath mixed with gritty water. The resulting series of coughs meant that whatever air I had managed to take in had gone.

I flailed my arms about hoping to be able to grab something. No such luck. More water filled my mouth as I attempted to breathe.

Please don't let it end like this, I thought.

Just as I began to believe that I might drown, a hand seized the collar of my shirt and lifted me out of the water. Jedidiah plopped me on the ground as I hacked up a mixture of water and spit.

"Anything broken?" he asked.

I did a quick check and surmised that despite almost drowning, I came out unscathed. "No. Where are the others?"

"Over there." He pointed to a small enclave where Aunt Ethel and Jackie huddled together. Rachel stood a few feet away from them watching Jedidiah and me.

"Come on." Jedidiah helped me up and guided me back to Jackie and Aunt Ethel. Despite the trail being only two feet wide, we made it.

"Oh, Mellow darling, I thought we had lost you." Aunt Ethel wrapped her feather coat around my shoulders; the worry in her voice very evident.

I shivered in response.

CHAPTER 8

Sometime during the night the rain stopped. I slept fitfully as the cold was inescapable and we had all huddled in a small space. I watched as the sun peeked over the horizon. Water still flowed below, but Jedidiah assured us that it would disappear in a day or two now that the rain had ceased.

Something caught my attention. Carefully, I pulled out the map and studied it while looking at a strange rock that looked exactly like a buffalo's head. I couldn't believe it.

"What is it?" asked Jackie.

I pointed out the rock to her. "Does that look like the head of a buffalo to you?"

Jackie's narrowed eyes told me it did as she studied the rock intently.

"I think it does," said Aunt Ethel with excitement.

I laid the map before them. "Look, this means that we are on the right track. The buffalo head is the first marker. Next we need to travel northwest until we reach the edge of a hidden ravine."

"Hidden ravine?" asked Rachel.

"That's what the map says." I pointed at the markings on the old map. "It is supposed to be marked by the eagle."

"There are a lot of hidden ravines around here," said Jedidiah.

"Well, we have to look for it," I said. "It's either that or we turn back now."

"Absolutely not," said Aunt Ethel.

"But how are we to get to the other side?" asked Jackie.

The water below us still flowed freely and we had no way of crossing it.

Jedidiah got an idea. He took a rope from my aunt's bag. He tied one end around a tree before hopping to the other side of the small canyon and tying the other end around the boulder from the map. He tugged on it until it pulled tight.

After several moments I noticed the incline in the rope and realized what Jedidiah's idea involved. "No," I said. "This is crazy."

"Use your belts to slide across the rope to the other side," said Jedidiah.

I eyed the rope warily and the water below. If we lost our grip we'd be lost to the river. Of course, leave it to my Aunt Ethel to embrace a crazy idea like this.

She took off her belt and put it over the rope and hung onto both ends. With a bounce, she jumped off the edge and sailed to the other side where Jedidiah caught her.

Jackie flung her belt over the rope. "See you on the other side." She sped to the other end and landed safely.

Warily, I approached the rope and put my belt over it still afraid of falling into the water below. I had no desire to almost drown for the third time in my life. My hands turned white as I tightly gripped the belt.

"You going to stand here all day?" asked Rachel.

"Well—"

I never got to finish my thought as Rachel shoved me off the ledge and I careened to the other end. Cold air blasted my face and a series of screams escaped my mouth. Jedidiah's outstretched arm caught me as I reached the other end.

"You did alright," he said.

"How are we to get the rope?" asked Jackie.

"Like you need to ask," said Rachel as she appeared with the other end of the rope and coiled it.

The snorting of a horse caught our attention. I looked up and saw one of our horses standing nearby nibbling on some grass. Another walked up. "How did they survive the rainstorm?"

"Animals know how to take care of themselves. Not sure where the others are, but having two of them here is a good sign." He checked the packs attached to the saddle. "Looks like most of our supplies are here."

Jedidiah scanned the badlands. "Well come on," he said, "Northwest is that way and daylight is burning." He took the reins of the horses and led them onward with the rest of us trailing behind.

We found a narrow trail that stretched along the top

of the canyon. Though we had to walk single file, the trek went fairly smoothly. Idle chatter filled our traveling and for a moment I thought that the worst of our trip was behind us. I couldn't have been more wrong.

Soft stomping stopped us in our tracks as we crested over a hill. The agitation of the horses told me that we had stumbled upon something that didn't bode well. Then, I saw it: a real live buffalo.

Its wooly, brown fur coated its body and I could tell it was thick. I had never seen a buffalo up close before and had no idea what to do. Nor did Jackie, Rachel, or Aunt Ethel. Jedidiah on the other hand was a different story.

"Nobody move," he said.

"Why not?" asked Jackie. "I thought buffalo were harmless."

"In storybooks," laughed Jedidiah. "This here is a wild buffalo and he's a bull. Just remain calm and back up slowly."

"But he's just a buffalo," said Rachel.

"Even in the wild they're dangerous and unpredictable," said Jedidiah. "And three of us are not ghosts."

The click of a camera caught our attention. Aunt Ethel had pulled out her brand new digital camera and snapped pictures repeatedly unconcerned that her actions might frighten the animal. Another click sounded as she took another picture.

"Quick, Mellow dear," said my aunt, "Get closer to it. I'll take your picture and you can show it to your friends when you get back home."

"Or post it at her funeral," muttered Jackie.

The camera took another picture.

"Come on, Mellow darling," said my aunt waving her arm, "don't disappoint an old lady."

"Ma'am," said Jedidiah, "you really might want to stop that."

My aunt took another picture.

The buffalo's head snapped up as it eyed my aunt. Vapor formed before its nostrils as it snorted in frustration.

I took a step back. Instantly, the buffalo jerked its head toward me forcing me to stop.

"Wow! This thing records video," said Aunt Ethel as she fiddled with her camera. "Maybe it was a good thing that I allowed that charming young man at the store to talk me into buying one of those SD cards as he called them. 32 GB. Whatever that means."

Aunt Ethel pointed her camera at all of us and did a scan capturing the entire situation on video.

"Here we are," narrated my aunt, "out in the wilds of the Dakotas face to face with a buffalo. Note the sternness of its scowl as it studies three people who clearly do not belong. Friend or foe he is asking himself."

"Aunt Ethel," I said, "please put your camera away." Even I noticed the buffalo becoming increasingly agitated.

Suddenly, the camera made a bunch of weird noises causing my aunt to lose her grip on it. Instinctively, she reached out to catch the camera and ended up juggling it as she tried to keep it from hitting the ground.

"There," she said as she finally got a firm grip on her new toy, "There are so many little buttons on here. Guess I'll have to read the instruction manual someday."

"Aunt Ethel, please," I hissed.

"Oh look, dear!" Something had caught Aunt Ethel's

attention forcing her to completely forget about the angry buffalo standing before us..

Undoubtedly having enough of our presence, the buffalo charged my aunt. It snorted violently as its hooves crashed into the frozen ground heading straight for my oblivious family member.

"Aunt Ethel, look out!" I screamed.

Jackie leapt for my aunt shoving her out of the way just in time. The painful scream she released told me that she had injured herself.

Jedidiah and Rachel leapt into action surrounding the animal and shouting at it. Confused, it tried ramming its horns into one of them but hit only thin air since they were both ghosts. Eventually, the thing became tired and confused and ran off.

"Jackie," I said as I bent down to examine her right ankle while she hugged it close.

"I think I broke it," said Jackie.

Carefully, I pulled up her pant leg. Broken or not, her ankle was definitely swollen. "Can you move it?"

Jackie managed to bend her ankle some, but not without excruciating pain.

"Don't worry, my dear," said Aunt Ethel as she waved her camera in front of Jackie, "I got the entire thing on here. Everyone will know of your harrowing ordeal and act of bravery."

Jackie seized Aunt Ethel's camera and smashed it against a rock. "You crazy—stupid—old—woman—GRRRR!"

Stunned, Aunt Ethel picked up the broken camera and opened it up. "Well, at least I know enough to keep the memory card intact." She stomped off.

"Jackie," I said, "Did you have to do that?"

The glare Jackie gave me told me that I should have kept my mouth shut.

"Well, the horses are still with us," said Jedidiah. "I guess we can turn back and she can ride one of them."

"We can't turn back," said Jackie.

"But your ankle," I said.

"We can't," repeated Jackie. "We're this close. And look!"

I watched as Jackie pulled back some weeds revealing a piece of artwork on a boulder protruding from the ground. I rubbed my fingers over it brushing away some of the grit that covered it. Sure enough, it was the marking of an eagle.

"Well give me some war paint and call me a Redskin," said Jedidiah. "That there is definitely the Indian depiction of an eagle. A mark of strength. And the second marker."

We all gaped at Jedidiah and his remark.

"What?" he said, confused.

"We don't say such things anymore," said Rachel, "as it's a bit insensitive."

"Insensitive?" said Jedidiah. "You all need to grow a stronger backbone. Should have heard some of the things people called me when I still breathed. And you—," he pointed at my aunt, "—what were you thinking with that contraption of yours? Didn't I tell you no sudden movements? A wild animal is still a wild animal."

"Hey!" My voice echoed off the canyons walls and effectively managed to shut everyone up. "We can debate 19th century slang versus the 21st century slang later. Jackie's ankle is starting to resemble a basketball here."

Jackie's ankle had increased in size some more. I had my reservations about continuing on, but this was one area where I got out voted. Both Jackie and my aunt agreed that we had to find Josiah Bard's treasure since we had stumbled upon the second marker.

"And lucky for you that we had the buffalo charge," said Aunt Ethel, "or we would never have found the second marker."

Jackie raised her hand to smack my aunt, but I seized it and forced her to put it down. Crazy or not she was still my aunt.

It became apparent that we weren't going anywhere anytime soon, we set up camp. Jedidiah scooped up some ice from an un-melted snow patch and wrapped it in a scarf; after which he placed it on Jackie's ankle. After the swelling had gone down some, he carefully wrapped it and put more ice it.

In an unusual truce, Aunt Ethel placed her coat on the ground to cushion Jackie's ankle as she elevated it. All the while, my aunt coveted that SD card as though it were some priceless relic while Jackie glowered at her with murderous eyes. Rachel had to play referee. A role that I think she enjoyed a bit too much.

"Jackie," I tried once more to convince her to turn back, "are you sure about going on? Your ankle—"

"I'll ride a horse," said Jackie in a tone that clearly indicated I was to drop the subject.

"What's the next clue on the map?" asked Rachel.

I pulled out the delicate paper and unfolded it. "According to this we are to head west until thunder roars beneath our feet."

"What kind of cockamamie instructions are those?" Rachel demanded. "Why can't they just say, 'Go here. Don't blow it all at once'"?

"As a test of our character," said Aunt Ethel. "Here we are out in the wild—" Aunt Ethel stopped talking when she noticed the look Jackie gave her. "Well," she continued, sheepishly, "they can't make it too easy for us to find it."

"What's next?" asked Jedidiah.

"After we find the thunder we are to follow the river," I said as I studied the map.

"Ain't no rivers around here that I know of," mused Jedidiah, "Unless it's underground. Well, you all better get some shut eye. It's bound to be a long day tomorrow."

CHAPTER 9

"Mel," said Jackie while the others slept, "Look at that sky."

I glanced at the star filled night sky having never seen so many of them before. The sky was littered with them and if I concentrated hard enough I could actually make out the Milky Way. It was definitely a beautiful sight.

"You don't get that in the city," said Jackie.

"No, you don't."

As I laid there on my back staring at the speckled sky, I realized why some people chose to live out here; why Jedidiah traveled here in the first place. The lack of people and city lights made it where you could appreciate nature, but live independently. The air was crisper and fresher and I didn't miss the smog of the city.

I wasn't sure if I could ever live in this vast open space, but kept it in mind in case my Aunt Ethel ever dropped by for another unannounced visit.

"How's the ankle?" I asked.

"Hurts," mumbled Jackie. "Seriously, don't worry about it. The swelling isn't so bad anymore. I'll just stay on the horse and you can do all the heavy lifting."

"What are friends for?" I joked.

"Can you two keep it down?" hissed Rachel, "How is a ghost to sleep?"

"Ghosts sleep?" said Jackie.

I shrugged and rolled over on my side where I promptly nodded off.

Morning came sooner than I wanted. Groggily, I sat up moaning from the aches and pains that racked my body from sleeping on a hard surface. I was starting to miss my bed. Or at least a soft mattress.

We ate a meager breakfast consisting of a few roots that Jedidiah had found and some of the dried stuff we had brought with us. My stomach growled wanting to eat more.

"Shut up," I told it.

With great effort, we managed to get Jackie on one of the horses. Three of us lifted her up carefully while trying to not touch her damaged ankle. A series of "Ows" told us that we were less than successful. Rachel stood on the other side of the horse to make certain that Jackie didn't fall off the other side. Twenty minutes later, we finally got her situated in the saddle.

"We need to move fast," said Jedidiah.

"Why's that?" asked Aunt Ethel.

"I think we're being tracked," replied Jedidiah.

"Tracked?" asked Aunt Ethel.

"Well who do you think was shooting at you a couple days ago? My guess is it wasn't target practice. Anyway, thought I heard someone or someone scrambling around while you all slept. Didn't find anything, but we ought to be careful just the same."

I had forgotten about the man that had taken pot shots at us when we first started out. Looking around, I could tell the others had too.

"How far until the next marker?" asked Jackie.

"The map doesn't give a distance," I replied. "It just says until we hear thunder beneath our feet."

"So we could easily be walking for the next two days," said Rachel.

"Could, but I doubt it," Jedidiah said, "Whoever made the map would not have wanted to be wandering these parts for long. He would have died of exposure. Or gotten lost himself."

I thought back to all the various canyons and trails that wove a maze in the earth. Getting lost out here was never far from my mind.

With the map in hand, and with Jedidiah's help, I led everyone onward. Aunt Ethel kept narrating our experience. For whose benefit was anyone's guess.

"Foraging our way through undiscovered country," continued my aunt.

Jackie snatched something and raised it with the

intention of smacking my aunt on the head. She stopped when I gave her a reproachful glare. Slowly, she put it down and released a sigh.

Sporadic snow flurries marked our trek downward into another ravine. The bitter wind chilled me as we moved. Repeatedly, I blew on my hands to warm them up. March was turning into a very cold month.

I had no idea how much time passed, but had the feeling that we were getting close to something. An object caught my attention. I grabbed it. The feel of the fabric told me that it was modern and therefore had been left there recently. Nope, we were not the only ones looking for the lost treasure of the Dakotas.

I showed the fabric chunk to the others.

"Someone's been through here before us," said Jackie. "But who?"

"Gil and Stark," I replied. "Remember they were gathering all of those digging tools and disappeared the morning we did. They were also the only other people to ask about the map and treasure besides us and Michael Evans."

"So you think they killed that Evans guy?" asked Jackie.

"Who else knows about the treasure? And how else would they get the map?" I asked.

It made sense, but at the same time it didn't. Those two didn't strike me as much for brains, but sometimes people get very good at putting on an act.

"I have my doubts about those two being murderous thieves," said Aunt Ethel.

"Hate to say it," added Jackie, "but I agree with your aunt on this one."

I let the scrap of fabric drop and be carted away by the wind. Perhaps they were right. I decided to forget about the murder and focus on the map and the gold.

The sun moved across the sky and more clouds rolled in with more flurries. It was one of those days where the sun could never make up its mind if wanted to stay out and the clouds kept trying to block it. Dreary and cold, we kept moving just to keep warm.

Aunt Ethel had grown tired of narrating our experiences and resorted to humming to herself. I had no idea what song she sang, but it sounded like a cheery tune. After a while, she decided to belt out some lyrics We all cringed as her voice carried over the landscape.

"HOME, HOME ON THE RANGE—" sang my aunt.

"Will you cut it out," scolded Rachel who had grown tired of Aunt Ethel's talking and singing. She voiced what we had all been thinking.

"I was just trying to lighten the mood," quipped Aunt Ethel.

I heard something. It sounded a bit faint, but it also sounded familiar. "Hush," I said.

"Mellow darling," said my aunt, "it is not polite to hush people."

"Shut up!" Immediately, I regretted saying that to Aunt Ethel. She pursed her lips and a scowl took over her face. "I'm sorry," I apologized, "but can you all hear that?"

Silence ensued as everyone paused trying to make out what I thought I heard.

I walked a bit farther with everyone close behind.

The noise grew louder. Straining my ears, I blocked out all other sounds as I listened intently. Sure enough, it sounded like thunder; thunder under my feet. The map had been right.

"It's here!" I shouted. "Listen."

The others listened and by their expressions I knew they heard it too.

"Thunder underground," breathed Aunt Ethel. "By golly there probably is an underground river. But, how do we find it?"

As though in answer to her question, I fell right through the ground as I took a step forward. Dust and dirt rained down upon me as I crashed onto a hard, rocky surface.

"Mel! Mel!" screamed Jackie.

"I'm fine," I called back rubbing my sore butt. I knew a few bruises were going to form. "I need a flashlight."

One landed beside me. I picked it up and scanned the area allowing the narrow beam to illuminate everything. It turned out that I stood upon a sort of riverbank and right next to me was the river. I found a stick and used it to test the depth of the water. Only about five inches disappeared beneath the surface so I surmised that the river was not very deep.

Another swoop with the flashlight revealed a small waterfall. I walked over to it. Carefully, I focused the light on it trying to see if there was some kind of opening above it. Nothing. I had no idea where the source of the water was, but in the end it didn't matter.

"Mel!"

I ran back to the hole I had fallen through. "I'm alright. There is an underground river and I believe it is the one the map meant for us to follow. But I cannot find another way down."

"Don't worry about it," said Jedidiah.

He lowered a rope and assisted Aunt Ethel as she clambered down to where I stood. Rachel appeared beside me with a smug expression.

"What about Jackie?" I said. "There's no way she can walk."

"Don't worry about me," said Jackie. She had climbed off the horse and limped over to the hole in the ground. "I'll stay with the horses and make sure they don't run off."

A part of me hated this plan. What if something happened?

"I guess Jedidiah can stay with you," I said.

"No," replied Jackie. "You're the one that tends to find trouble. I'll be fine on my own."

Reluctantly, I agreed to her wishes. We walked downriver as the map had instructed. For all of us to move together, we ended up walking in the river itself which wasn't difficult since the water only came up to our ankles. The river resembled a creek more than anything else and the water was more lukewarm than cold; something I hadn't expected..

We walked as quietly as we could unsure of what we would find. This also meant that Aunt Ethel ceased her narrating and singing, much to our relief. That old woman could drive anyone crazy. Sometimes I considered shipping her off to Congress. They'd probably do their job just to be rid of her. If anything, it would get her out of my hair for a while. Okay, maybe it sounds mean, but I dare anyone to spend a week with her.

Voices echoing ahead of us snapped our attention. From a distance, I easily deciphered that they belonged to Gil and Stark. Something metal clattered on the ground.

"Not that way you idiot," scolded Stark. "Now hand me the shovel."

Gil handed him the pick.

"No, that's the shovel, this is a pick." Stark threw the pick to the ground.

Gil walked over to get the shovel, but tripped over his own two feet and crashed into the dirt.

"If they killed that Evans fella," said Rachel, "then I'm your Aunt Ethel."

Gil and Stark finally noticed us and stopped cold. "What are you doing here?" they demanded.

"I could ask the same of you," I said. "Did you kill Michael Evans?" So, not the most tactful way of putting it, but it's to the point.

"No," said Stark. "We never knew him."

"Besides, we're too stupid to do something like that," added Gil. I don't think what he said registered in his brain.

Rachel busted up laughing. "You got that part right!"

"Then why did you come to the ranch?" I demanded, ignoring Rachel's guffawing. "You two don't strike me as country people."

"We heard about the legend of Josiah Bard. Found it by accident during a web search. So we decided to come out here and look for it."

"How did you come upon the map?" asked Aunt Ethel.

"We found it," said Gil, "Honest. We happened to find it on the stairwell of the lodge. But we never killed anyone to get it."

"That means someone else killed Michael Evans and is after the treasure," muttered Rachel.

"Give us the gold and we'll be on our way," I said.

"Are you crazy?" said Gil. "We found it first."

"Perhaps it escaped your notice, but someone killed that Evans guy for the map. That means he will probably kill whomever has the treasure," I said.

Gil and Stark looked at each other before looking at me.

I hadn't noticed Rachel moving to the side where a bunch of bags were. She, like myself, must have guessed that the gold was in them. Suddenly, Rachel snatched a bag and took off down the tunnel. "Run! I got it! I got it!"

Gil and Stark rushed to the other bags while Aunt Ethel and I turned and ran with Jedidiah close behind. Of course, all the two idiots saw was a bag careening down the cavern with a disembodied voice screaming. In all the mayhem I never noticed that they hadn't followed us.

"Rachel, stop," I said. "Stop!"

"What?" asked Rachel as she slowed to a halt.

I took the bag from her and opened it. Nothing but packages of jerky and bottles of water were in it. "Congratulations. You just stole a bag of food."

Rachel jerked the bag out of my hands. "Unbelievable. Those two tricked me."

"Rachel—"

"I'm going to get them." Rachel disappeared.

"That certainly explains why they weren't following us," said Aunt Ethel.

A series of frightened screams echoed around us as they bounced off the walls. I turned around. Gil and Stark both ran toward us with a couple of bulging sacks and a shovel chasing after them.

"I'll beat you both to a pulp," shouted Rachel.

"Get it away from us," yelled Stark.

"Help us," shouted Gil.

They dropped their bags by our feet and both hid behind me.

"Rachel, please," I said.

She stopped chasing the two men but remained nearby with the shovel in her hands.

I scooped up one of the bags. Inside was a variety of items: some of it made from gold, letters, journals, a few rolls of money, a gun dating back to the 1800s, and a few other items I didn't know. "Is this the treasure?"

Gill and Stark nodded. "It's what we found."

"Not much in the way of treasure," said Rachel.

"I don't think so," I replied, "Some of this you could sell to a collector for a lot of money. These journals would be of immense value to any historical society."

"Mel!"

Jackie's voice echoed throughout the caverns. By the tone I knew she was in trouble.

"You obviously don't need us," said Gil.

Rachel waved the shovel at him and he and Stark shied away from it.

"Mel!"

I took off with the bags and the others close behind. It didn't take long for me to reach the hole in the ceiling where I had fallen through.

"Mel!"

"Jackie!," I shouted as I reached the hole.

"Hold it right there," said a harsh voice. Peering into the sunlight, I noticed it was Poppy. He held Jackie by the neck with a gun pointed at her.

"I'll take care of him," said Rachel.

"No," I hissed. "What if that gun goes off and hits Jackie?"

Huffing, Rachel remained where she was.

"Mellow Summers I presume," said Poppy. "I know you have the treasure. Do not bother denying it. If you wish to see your friend again, be at that made up town on the ranch by noon tomorrow with the gold."

"Noon! It took us three days to get here."

"Be there at noon, or say good-bye to your friend."

"But—"

Poppy disappeared with Jackie. I heard her scream and struggle until she fell silent and only the galloping of hooves remained as they slowly faded.

"How could I have let this happen?" I asked.

"Mel," said Rachel.

"It's all my fault!"

"No, it's not," said Aunt Ethel. "It's no one's fault. We'll just have to be at the town tomorrow like he says."

"But won't there be people there?" asked Rachel.

"That place is usually empty on Sundays," said Jedidiah. "That man reminds me of an Indian that used to roam these parts. Mean son of a bitch. He didn't like people being in his territory. Didn't matter if they were Indian or white. If you wandered into his territory, he killed you."

I just stared at Jedidiah wondering what the point of his story was. Who cares about some Indian that lived over 130 years ago when Jackie's life was in danger?

"The proper term is Native American," said Gil. I guess he not only heard Jedidiah, but saw him as well. It was Rachel who remained invisible while still holding the shovel.

"He was no more native to this land than I was," said Jedidiah, "And it doesn't matter what the proper term is. I have spent the last thirty years watching people come out to this Dude Ranch, as you call it, with their fancy gadgets, strange dress, and snobbish attitudes. They think that by coming out here for a week they are learning what it was like to settle this land.

"In my day the only heat you got was from the kindling you were able to gather. Your food was what you killed or managed to grow. There was no relief from the heat in the summer. Water was what you could dig out of the ground not something you bought at a store.

"You modern folk think you know so much with your gadgets and fancy reading material. You think that those of us who left our comfortable homes in the east and came out here did so because we wanted to kill Indians or rob them. Well, I got news for you. Those of us who came here were looking for a better life. We had nothing back home after the war and we just wanted to be left alone. I came out here after some carpetbagger conned me out of my savings and a bunch of drunken Yankees burned what property I had left.

"When I came to these parts I found a harsh and uninviting land that was colder than the ice queen herself. The people who settled here had to be just as tough. My first winter here I came upon an Indian boy. He had gotten caught in a blizzard and separated from his family. His foot had turned black and I brought him to the nearest outpost where the surgeon amputated it.

"Sometime later, I was out trapping animals when a blizzard sprang up. It was mid-January and I should have known better. Two days I wandered around until I could walk no more. A few days later that same Indian boy found me, though he had become a man by then. He must have recognized me because he returned the favor by bringing me to the nearest Calvary outpost.

"Of course by then both my legs had turned black and were amputated. I remember every bit of it. I died a few days later from infection. You want to know who stayed by my bed the entire time? That Indian boy. He even said the words at my funeral.

"So don't you ever try to brand me as some Indian hater. I know more about their ways and have more respect for them that you will ever have. The only thing you know about them is probably what you've seen on that box with the moving pictures.

"Now you may not have liked my story about the murdering Redskin, but the moral is the same. That Poppy character is just like the Indian that hunted people down for pleasure. Do you honestly think he will let any of you live once he gets the gold? He ain't going to risk letting you turn him into the law."

"So what are you saying?" I asked.

"It's a trap," replied Jedidiah. "You give him those bags and he will kill you and your friend."

"So what do we do?" I asked.

"Well first, I need to get up there and get that rope so you can get out. Unless those two remember how they got down here."

Gil and Stark looked at each and shrugged their shoulders. "We don't remember," said Stark. "We ended up down here by a happy circumstance."

"So how were you going to get out with the gold?" asked Aunt Ethel.

"Uh, we didn't think that far ahead," said Gil.

"Yeah, Gil here got lost in his own closet once," said Stark.

"That doesn't surprise me," said Rachel.

Jedidiah shook his head. "The Lord must love stupid people. He makes a lot of 'em." He disappeared and moments later the rope lowered itself down.

"Jesus it's a ghost!" shouted Gil as he jumped back. "It's a ghost—a real live ghost!"

"Can I please just hit him once with this shovel?" pleaded Rachel.

As tempting as it was I replied with a soft, "No."

Rachel chucked the shovel to the ground which hit Gil in the foot. "Oops," she said in a not so innocent tone.

I gave her a reproachful look.

"It slipped," said Rachel.

We each clambered up the rope. The horses remained where we had left them.

"So what's the plan?" I asked.

"Obviously, we need to get the sheriff to the town," said Aunt Ethel, "Though I do not know how that is possible short of Rachel kidnapping him."

Rachel's face brightened at that prospect. "Kidnap the sheriff! That is a brilliant idea. I've never done that before and the best part is they can't arrest me cuz I'm already dead."

"Rach—" I tried to say, but she had already disappeared.

"How are we to get to that town by noon tomorrow?" asked Aunt Ethel.

"Poppy probably knows a short cut back now that he knows where the treasure was," said Jedidiah. "Thing is, I know one too. If we ride through the night we should be able to make it."

"What about those two?" I asked pointing at Gil and Stark who each had resorted to picking their noses.

Jedidiah sighed. "I guess leaving them here would be cruel and unusual punishment. They'll have to come with us. And we'll have to double up on the horses."

CHAPTER 10

We ended up riding through the entire night not even stopping to rest our horses. Turned out that when we discovered the underground river, Jedidiah recognized some of the landmarks and knew right away where we were and how to get back to the ranch quickly. Short cut after short cut and we managed to crawl out of the Badlands around sunrise. After that we rode hard across the plains to the "Old West Town" that the ranch owner had built for his guests.

I felt my horse tiring underneath me as we rode. Even I was exhausted, but stopping was not an option. Jackie's life hung in the balance and I knew that if we managed to make it out of the canyons in a short time, Poppy did too. Just before noon we came upon the town. Jedidiah stopped us before we got too close.

"What is it?" I asked.

"Remember what I said about the trap?"

I nodded my head.

"You are going to ride in there alone with these bags." Jedidiah handed me the bags containing the buried treasure. "The rest of us will position ourselves around the town and hide. One of us will cause a distraction. When that happens, you get Jackie out of there."

"Why do I have to ride in alone?" I asked, "Won't he be expecting all of us."

"I have to agree with, Mellow," said Aunt Ethel.

"I doubt he'll be expecting those two," Jedidiah pointed at Gil and Stark, "And he doesn't know about me. As for you, ma'am, he won't be expecting an old woman to be able to ride through the night.

"Sending, Mel, in alone should set him at ease and she was the one he was talking about."

The plan sounded solid enough. Where was Rachel? I had hoped she would be here already, but she seemed to be running late. After the others disappeared, I rode into town.

I felt like I had actually traveled into a western movie as the horse's hooves clopped on the ground with slow, determined movements. I adjusted my cowboy hat slightly to shade my eyes from the bright midday sun. The clouds from the day before seemed to have vanished into thin air. Looking around, I didn't see any sign of Poppy.

Once I reached the middle of town, I dismounted and tied my horse to one of the rails. Carefully, I placed the bags on my shoulder and walked into the middle of the dirt road. An image of two cowboys with cigarettes hanging out of their mouths meeting at high noon for a duel filtered through my mind. Where was Poppy?

"Hold it right there," said Poppy as he appeared from an alley.

Well that answered that question.

I stopped. I watched him strut out into the middle of the road dragging Jackie behind. The look of pain in her face told me that her ankle had gotten worse during this ordeal.

"You alone?" demanded Poppy as he held a gun to Jackie's head.

"Yes," I replied.

"I don't believe you."

"My aunt is in her sixties and can hardly move that fast. And you have the third member of our party so you do the math."

"Toss the bags to me," said Poppy.

"Let Jackie go first," I said.

"Toss me the bags or say good-bye to your friend." I heard the click as Poppy cocked the gun.

Knowing there was nothing else for me to do, I threw the bags to his feet. "You have the gold, now let Jackie go."

"You must think I'm really stupid," said Poppy.

Actually, I had a few other words in mind for what I thought of him. "Look, you have what you wanted now let her go."

"You know I won't," said Poppy, "No witnesses."

My heart sank. Things were happening exactly as Jedidiah had said they would.

"Your aunt will probably die out there in those canyons. You and her though will be another matter. By the time they find your bodies out here, there won't be much of them left."

Suddenly, a series of pops that sounded like gun shots went off. It turned out to be firecrackers, but it served as a big enough distraction. Poppy whirled around in surprise. Using this chance Jackie smashed her fists into Poppy's face at the same time that I tackled him.

Quickly, I grabbed Jackie and yanked her to her feet ignoring her yelps of pain. Poppy fired his gun at us. Bits of wood splintered in our direction as the bullet hit a nearby building just as I pulled Jackie around the corner. I searched for a place to put her until we could subdue Poppy. It turned out, that I needn't have worried.

Sirens echoed around us as a bunch of cop cars careened into the town. Sheriff Judson spilled out of the lead car dazed and a bit confused. I noticed Rachel in the driver's seat. The car itself had a crumpled hood, a flat tire, and a broken windshield. Way to go Rachel.

Poppy turned and opened fire upon the sheriff and his deputies who promptly returned fire. Then, out of nowhere a flying feather coat headed straight for Poppy.

"Shoot my Mellow, will you?" shouted Aunt Ethel as she crashed into the stunned Poppy and knocked his gun out of his hands. She wrenched him off the ground, placed him over her knee, and spanked him. I don't know how she did it, but that woman had some muscle.

Rachel walked up with a metal bar and placed it in my aunt's hands. Of course, all Poppy saw was a metal bar floating through midair to my aunt. His wide eyes said it all.

"I'll teach you to attack my Mellow," scolded Aunt Ethel as she hit Poppy with the metal bar. "And what about that Michael Evans, did you kill him?"

"Yes! Yes! Let me go you crazy old bat!"

Poppy managed to knock my aunt over and sprinted for freedom. He didn't count on Rachel, however. She tripped the man and he crashed into Sheriff Judson who quickly put him in handcuffs.

"Poppy, I'm arresting you for the murder of Michael Evans, for kidnapping, and attempted murder. You have the right to remain silent..."

The sheriff finished reading Poppy his rights as Jackie and I walked over. Well, Jackie hobbled while leaning on my shoulder. I handed her over to Aunt Ethel as I picked up the bags with the buried treasure.

"Here," I said handing the bags to the sheriff, "This is the fabled treasure of the badlands. We found it before Poppy tried to take it."

Sheriff Judson took the bags. "I distinctly remember telling you to not try and solve this case."

"I didn't," I said, "I set out on a treasure hunt which just happened to result in the solving of a murder."

"Actually," began Gil, "we—"

Rachel slapped her hand over Gil's mouth shutting him up. He jumped back from being struck by seemingly nothing.

"I'll need you all to come down to the sheriff's office and give your statements," said Sheriff Judson, "But first I'll have one of my deputies take you to the doctor's office to get that ankle looked at."

He waved one of his deputies over. I told Aunt Ethel that I would meet her back at the ranch house after we took care of Jackie's ankle.

"So," said Rachel.

"So," I whispered not wanting to be talking to thin air.

"Aren't you going to ask how I got the sheriff here?"

"Not really."

"Well, I'll tell you anyway," said Rachel, "First, I had to track him, which actually took a while. That man can be difficult to find. Finally, I found him. I threw him into the passenger seat of his car, crashed it into one of his deputies' vehicles so that they would chase us. Then, I high tailed it out here. Great work, right?"

"Yeah," I said. What else do you tell a ghost that is extremely proud of herself? "You saved our bacon. Look, I'll meet you back at the ranch later. I need to get Jackie to the doctor."

"Sure you don't want me to come along?"

"I think I can handle it."

I crawled into the car with Jackie as Rachel waved to us.

CHAPTER 11

I zipped up my suitcase relieved that the vacation was over. I carefully wrapped my camera. I never did get anything done on my Independent Study project. That meant when I got home I'd have to work double time to get it done.

The doctor had fixed up Jackie's ankle pretty good. Turned out she had only cracked the bone, but she still had to have a cast on it for the next month. He was a kindly old gentleman and I really liked him. He even gave us all the paperwork and his notes on everything he did to give to her doctor when we got back home.

I stepped toward my closet to finish packing my things. "No!" yelled Jackie. "Step away from the closet."

"Jackie, I—"

"You are not opening that." Jackie stumbled across the room; her cast thumping on the floor. She squeezed between me and the closet door. "The last time you opened your closet in this place, a dead body fell out. We are not taking any chances."

"Jackie, don't be silly."

I reached past her and wrenched the door open. Out fell Rachel with her eyes closed and holding a white lily. She fell to the floor landing on her back making a good imitation of a dead man.

"See what I mean?" I said, "It's nothing we can't live without. We'll just shove her back in there and go."

"Hey," said Rachel, "Show some respect for the dead." She hopped to her feet dropping the lily.

Aunt Ethel burst into our room. "Mellow darling, you must see this."

"When did you get an iPad?" I asked, noticing the electronic object in her hands.

"Oh, a while back," said my aunt, "This nice young man in an electronic store said that it was an essential component of modern living. Almost forgot that I had it. Now look at this"

Aunt Ethel placed the iPad in front of Jackie and I. On it played the recorded video of how Jackie braved the buffalo, saved my aunt, and broke her ankle. It even captured the look of pure terror that had covered her face.

"And when I get back home, I am going to place it on that YouTube," said Aunt Ethel, "Someone showed me how."

"Wasn't me," blurted out Rachel.

"I'm sure the public will appreciate it," I said.

Jackie's pinched face told me not only was she beyond angry, but that I should have kept my mouth shut.

I finished packing my luggage. Jackie and I really needed to hit the road. "Well, Aunt Ethel," I said, "it was a pleasure seeing you again, but we need to get going."

"Oh, Mellow dear, can't you stay a little longer?"

"We really need to get back." I kissed my aunt on the cheek and bent down to pick up Jackie's and my bags. Just as I reached for them, they picked themselves up and hovered in midair.

"I can take those," said Jedidiah. "Least I can do after what you ladies have been through."

Not arguing with him, we followed him out into the hallway where we ran right into Miss Hollywood, or Liz.

"Excuse me," she said in a rude tone as Jedidiah accidentally bumped into her.

"Well, I'm sorry, ma'am," said Jedidiah, tipping his hat.

"You almost made me ruin my pedicure."

I studied the woman in her designer sports bra and exercise pants and flip flops. Now, I knew what Jedidiah had meant when he called us modern folk spoiled. Ruin her pedicure? Give me a break. Does that woman think about anything other than her appearance?

"It cost me like $200," continued the woman.

"Sorry to hear that," replied Jedidiah, "Seems like a waste of money if you ask me." He proceeded down the hall and disappeared. For the first time, the woman noticed the suitcases moving on their own.

Rachel got a devilish grin on her face. Remaining

invisible, she ran right into Miss Hollywood causing her to crash into one of the planters and get potting soil all over her. "Oops, my bad," said Rachel.

The woman looked at all of us trying to figure out what just happened. Fuming, she screamed and smacked the floor with her fists.

The rest of us just walked away. I certainly didn't feel sorry for her.

Once the car was packed up, Jackie and I pulled out onto the dirt road and headed for the highway. Aunt Ethel said she wanted to stay a few extra days, which was fine with me.

We found the highway easily enough. I was actually beginning to learn my way around the area. Unfortunately, twenty minutes after we did, a state trooper pulled us over. Oh curse Tiny and the naked lady he painted on my car. And just my luck, it was the same state trooper that had pulled me over when I had first arrived.

"License and registration please," he said as he reached the driver's side.

"Officer, I wasn't even speeding," I said. And I wasn't.

"You were doing well below the speed limit," he said.

You had got to be kidding me. "I was only doing five below that hardly justifies a ticket. What is this quota time?"

I knew I should have kept my big mouth shut, but this was ridiculous.

"Step out of the car please," said the trooper.

"Don't do it," said Rachel materializing in the back seat. "Tell him to buzz off."

"Rachel, I can't just—"

"Why'd he pull you over?" demanded Rachel.

"For doing five below the limit," answered Jackie.

"What is this quota season?" said Rachel. "Tell him to take a hike."

"Rachel, if I do that I'll get arrested," I said.

The trooper watched our exchange with interest and bewilderment. He couldn't see or hear Rachel. "Uh, ma'am, I need you to step out of the car."

"Not once Jedidiah gets through with him," said Rachel, "He says this guy is a class A jerk. Likes to pull women over, if you know what I mean."

"Where is Jedidiah?" I asked.

In answer to my question, the state trooper's car turned itself on and sped down the highway with the lights going.

"Yee-Haw!" shouted Jedidiah through an open window.

The trooper watched his car drive itself. "Hey! That's my—" he stopped talking when he realized that no one sat in the driver's seat; well, no one but a ghost. The trooper chased after his vehicle.

"Just go," said Rachel.

The trooper's car did a U-turn and sped past us again.

"I ain't ever been behind one of these contraptions," shouted Jedidiah as he waved at us.

I watched as the trooper ran by us cursing his car as it continued down the highway.

"What if he—" I began.

"What's he going to do?" said Rachel, "Tell his captain that his car drove itself while he was trying to give you a ticket?"

The distinct crunch of metal against a tree reached our ears.

"Or that it crashed itself?" asked Rachel. "Believe me. He isn't going to want you around. Now go."

I started the car and drove away while the state trooper circled his car with a string of curses. That was one ticket I managed to avoid thanks to a couple of ghosts. I hoped the rest of our trip was uneventful.

"You know the next vacation we take," said Jackie, "is going to be Aunt Ethel free and in Florida with sandy beaches."

"OOO, we should go there now," said Rachel bouncing in the back seat, "I know the best Tiki Bar."

Okay, so maybe uneventful was a bit much to hope for.

Get book 7 in the series.

Two Ghosts Haunt A Grove

ABOUT THE AUTHOR

Janet McNulty currently resides in West Virginia where she moved after receiving her B.A. in History. She lives with her three cats who keep her on task.

When not writing, Ms. McNulty enjoys just lounging around outside or reading a variety of books by a multitude of authors.

More by Janet McNulty

The Mellow Summers Series

Sugar And Spice And Not So Nice
Frogs, Snails, And A Lot Of Wails
An Apple A Day Keeps Murder Away
Three Little Ghosts
Oh Holy Ghost
Where Trouble Roams
Two Ghosts Haunt A Grove
Trick Or Treat Or Murder
Roses Are Red…He's Dead
Double, Double Nothing But Trouble

Mellow Summers moves to Vermont to attend college, accompanied by her friend Jackie. They soon find themselves running into ghosts and one mystery after another.

The Dystopia Trilogy

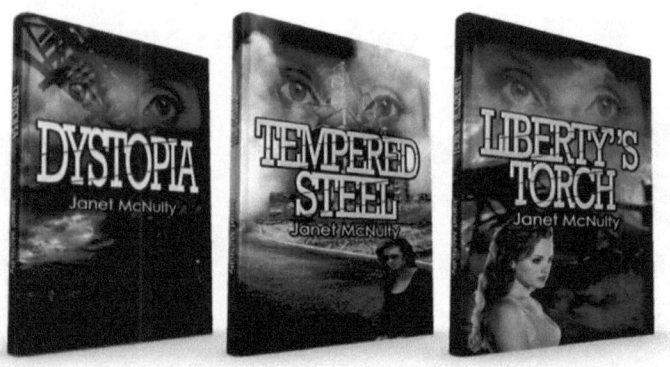

Dystopia (Book 1)
Tempered Steel (Book 2)
Liberty's Torch (Book 3)

**Imagine living in a world where
everything you do is controlled.**

Dana Ginary lives in a world where every aspect of her life is controlled by the Dystopian Government. Forced to work in Waste Management, her life becomes a nightmare with hunger and survival is her only constant. Before she knows it, she is caught up in a resistance movement and exiled from Dystopia, forced to find her way in the barren wastelands. While there, she must learn to live independently and discover how far she is willing to go to live and achieve freedom.

The Solaris Saga

Solaris Seethes
Solaris Seeks
Solaris Strays
Solaris Soars

Every myth has a beginning

After escaping the destruction of her home planet, Lanyr, with the help of the mysterious Solaris, Rynah must put her faith in an ancient legend. Never one to believe in stories and legends, she is forced to follow the ancient tales of her people: tales that also seem to predict her current situation.

Forced to unite with four unlikely heroes from an unknown planet (the philosopher, the warrior, the lover, the inventor) in order to save the Lanyran people, Rynah and Solaris embark on an adventure that will shatter everything Rynah once believed.

The Legends Lost Series

Published under Nova Rose

Tesnayr
Amborese
Galdin

Enter the Lands of Tesnayr and join on an epic fantasy adventure that spans over 1,500 years.

Begin with Tesnayr, the first king of the five lands as he unites the against a savage foe bent on their destruction.

Next, Join Amborese as she fights reclaim the throne after her family was forced to flee from it.

Thinking peace has finally entered the land, follow Galdin as he returns to Tesnayr to find it greatly hanged. Barbarians, led by a mysterious sorcerer, burn and destroy as they go. And only Galdin can stop them if he chooses to accept his fate.

Visit www.legendslosttrilogy.com to learn more about the Legends Lost Trilogy.

Grandpa's Stories

My grandfather grew up in Arizona during the 1920s and 1930s. One week after the attack on Pearl Harbor he joined the Navy. During the summer of 2012, my mother visited him and recorded his stories about growing up, World War II, and his time as an employee at the Pacific Bell Telephone Company. This is the history of the 20th century as he lived it. These recordings make up this book. These are his words.

www.ingramcontent.com/pod-product-compliance
Lightning Source LLC
Chambersburg PA
CBHW030536180626
46810CB00005B/1897